The Diary

of

Robin's Toys

Ken and Angie Lake

D1371960

Taffy the Rabbit

Published by Sweet Cherry Publishing Limited
53 St. Stephens Road,
Leicester, LE2 1GH
United Kingdom

First Published in the UK in 2013

ISBN: 978-1-78226-026-4
Text: © Ken and Angie Lake 2013
Illustrations: (c) Joyson Loitongbam,
Creative Books

Title: Taffy the Rabbit - The Diaries of Robin's Toys

Printed and Bound By Nutech Print Services, India

Every Toy Has a Story to Tell

Have you ever seen an old toy, perhaps in a cupboard, or in the attic or loft? Have you ever seen how sad they look at car boot sales, unwanted and unloved? Well, look at them closely, because every toy has a story to tell, and the older, the more decrepit, the more scruffy, the more tatty the toy is, the more interesting its story could be. Here are just a few of those toys and their stories.

24th June, 09.25

Saturday night had been windy, and the rattling windows had kept Robin awake. He guessed that there had been a storm, or even a gale. He wasn't sure what the difference was.

But on Sunday morning the weather was calm again. After breakfast, as he opened the curtains and looked out at the street, he could see the damage that the wind had done.

Mr Brown's fence had
blown down and the dustbins
were on their sides. The rubbish

had blown all down the street, and poor old Mrs Brown was out there trying to pick it up.

Robin noticed that the dead leaves had blown into little piles beside every door, and there were pieces of newspaper scattered around.

Robin was doodling with a pencil on a piece of paper as he waited for Grandad to arrive. He drew some trees and a tent, and children around a campfire.

Robin had had some bad news that week. He was in the Boy Scouts, and all year they'd been looking forward to their summer camping trip.

Every summer since he'd become a Scout the boys would all get together and spend a week living with nature, camping in tents, learning to fish, singing songs by the campfire at night...

And on the last night, when the Scout Leaders were asleep, they would all creep into one tent and have a secret midnight feast!

But this year it would be different. At the last meeting they were all supposed to prepare the camping equipment and make sure everything was there, but when they unpacked the equipment... Oh dear! The tents must have been put back without being cleaned last year, as they were all wet and covered in mud. The canvasses were mouldy and rotten, and tore as they unpacked them, and all the tent poles had gone rusty!

In fact, the camping equipment had needed replacing for years, but there was never enough money. So they always made do, sewing up the

odd hole in the canvasses and groundsheets. But this year there would be no more making do; everything was useless.

Steve Whitehouse was the Scout Leader. He had worked himself up into a real frenzy, trying to salvage whatever he could, but there weren't enough good bits to put together a single tent.

"Well, boys," he said, looking very disappointed, "I'm afraid that unless some kind person donates some equipment, there'll be no summer camp this year."

The boys were devastated. Robin had been stashing away chocolate bars and crisps for weeks, looking forward to the midnight feast.

Robin was so lost in his thoughts that he didn't even notice Grandad's little red car turn into the street.

Beep, beep! Beep, beep!

"Come on, Robin, it's Sunday morning and time to go to the car boot sale."

"Thank you, Grandad."

"How has your week been, Robin?"

"I have been working really hard revising. We have exams coming up and I want to do well to make Mum and Dad, and you and Grandma, really proud of me."

"I am sure we will be proud just to know that you are trying so hard."

"And I was really looking forward to Scout camp, but it's been cancelled."

"Oh, that is a shame, Robin, I know how much you love summer camp. Never mind, let's see if we can find a toy at the car boot sale to cheer you up!"

"How's Grandma?"

"She was in the garden when I left. She said something about trying to mend the water sprinkler system I installed last week. Lovely weather for it this morning."

The car boot sale was busy that morning. There were lots and lots of stalls, and lots of

people looking for bargains.
Egburt's Electrics was there, a
real sign that summer was here.

Old Egburt bought
electrical appliances that the
warehouses couldn't sell or that
had been returned by the shops.
They would have a big clear-out

once a year and he would buy boxes of stuff. Once he had sold it all, he wouldn't come back to the car boot sale until the next warehouse clearance.

This suited Egburt, because it meant that people couldn't bring the faulty stuff back to him.

Grandad wanted to have a look for something for Grandma. She deserved a nice present, because she was always making such wonderful cakes.

"What do you think, Robin? Do you have any ideas for what we could get your grandma?"

"I'm not really sure; shall we have a look around the car boot sale while we think about it?"

"That's a good idea," said Grandad. "Okay, Robin, here is your 50 pence to buy a toy. Now where shall we start today?"

"I don't know, Grandad.
Let's just wander around for a
while until we find something
interesting."

So that's what they did.

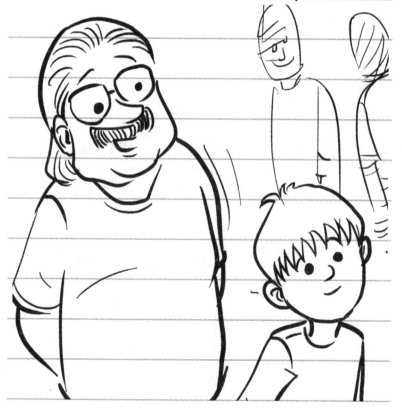

They looked at most of the stalls, but didn't find any toys which were really different or interesting.

"That's a bit disappointing, Grandad."

"Wait a minute, Robin. We didn't see Jason's Jumble, did we?"

"No, you are right, Grandad, we must have missed that one."

So they went around again, and there was the stall right in the corner, almost hidden from view.

"Good morning, Mr Jumble. We are looking for an interesting toy; you know, one with a bit of history. Do you have anything like that?"

"Do I have a toy with history? Well, young man, I certainly do. You have come to the right place this morning."

He reached into an old hat
and pulled out a smiling rabbit.

"There, how is that for a
rabbit-out-of-a-hat trick? This
is Taffy, and as I am sure you
have guessed, he is a Welsh
rabbit."

Taffy was dressed in a little pair of red shorts, and was wearing a red top with a dragon on it and a number 9 on the back.

"As you can see, Taffy is a real sporting rabbit, and he loves rugby. I have a feeling that he may have played for Wales once."

Robin looked at Grandad,
and Grandad winked back at him.

"Yes, Mr Jumble, I like the
look of Taffy. How much is he?"

"How much have you got?"

"I only have 50 pence. Is that going to be enough?"

"Alright, son. As it's you,

and as I like rugby as well, you can have him for 50 pence. Shall I put Taffy the Rabbit in a bag for you?"

They were both happy with the purchase, so Grandad and Robin continued walking around to find a present for Grandma.

They ended up back at
Egburt's Electrics, where
Grandad found just what he was
looking for.

After a successful morning, they jumped into the little red car and made their way back to Grandad's house, where, as happened every Sunday, they were greeted by the delicious smell of fresh baking.

"Hmm, oh yes, Grandma! Something smells very nice!" said Robin as he rushed in through the front door.

"Hello, boys! While you were out I made you a nice fruit cake to have with your tea. Did you have a good morning at the car boot sale?"

"Oh thank you, Grandma, I love your fruit cake! Yes, we had a great time."

Grandad gave Grandma the bag with her present inside and she examined the contents.

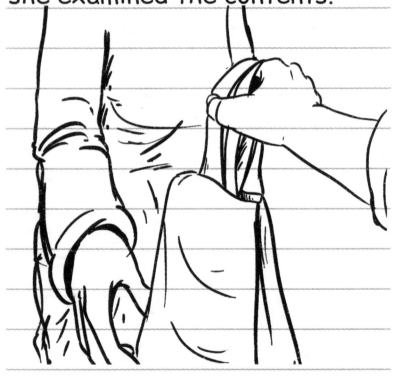

"What is it?" she asked.

"Ah," said Grandad. "That, my dear, is an alarm clock ... but not just any old alarm clock. That one will work up to 300 feet underwater."

"Oh, that's wonderful, Harry," said Grandma. "That will come in really handy on our next holiday in the lost city of Atlantis!"

"I knew you would like it, dear," said Grandad.

"Right, boys, I'm going to potter in the garden for a bit. I'll see you later."

When Grandma had gone, they put Taffy on the kitchen table and Grandad said his magic spell.

"Little toy, hear this rhyme,
Let it take you back in time,
Tales of sadness or of glory,
Little toy, reveal your story."

Taffy blinked, stretched his front legs, wiggled his nose, twitched his whiskers and yawned.

"Hello, who are you two?"

"I am Robin, and this is my grandad."

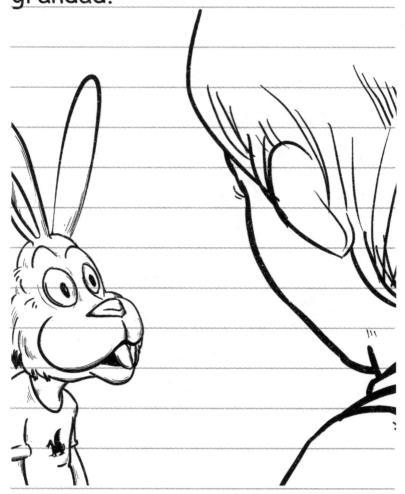

"Oh right. I am very pleased to meet you. My name is Taffy."

"Yes, we know."

"Do you know anything about rabbits, or rugby, or Wales?"

"Not much, but we'd love to learn!" said Robin.

"Alright, if you are both sitting comfortably, I shall tell you a little bit about all three. First of all, rabbits.

"Well, we are mammals and covered in fur. A boy rabbit is called a buck, and a girl rabbit is called a doe. Do you know what a young rabbit is called?"

"Err no, Taffy, I don't think we do."

"I shall tell you then. They are called kittens or kits. We live in groups underground in burrows, and a collection of burrows is called a warren.

"I think that's all you need to know about us, except that we can run very quickly. I am one of the fastest runners in Rabbit School. Anyway, let me tell you a bit about Wales.

"I am a Welsh rabbit and very proud of it. I love my national identity and talk about it whenever I can. If you are not sure where Wales is, it's the big bit which sticks out to the left of England.

"You see, the true Welsh were a nation of Celts who gradually did a sideways move when England was invaded by other cultures - far too many to mention in this story.

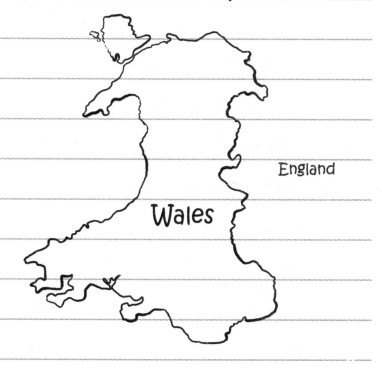

"So the Welsh became concentrated in Wales, which makes sense. The Welsh have their own ancient language; it sounds very beautiful. It is spoken mainly in North Wales, that's the bit at the top. But not all Welsh people can speak it. And as for Welsh rabbits, well, they even have problems speaking English.

"The Welsh have lots of choirs and they love to sing, but don't assume that all Welsh people have good singing voices.

Have you ever heard of a Welsh rabbit choir? No, me neither!

"Alright, now let me tell you about Rugby Union. I know that it started in England at Rugby School, but we don't mention that. In Wales it's not just thought of as a game, it's taken very seriously!

"There is a lot of national pride about it. There are fifteen men on each side, and they can only pass the ball backwards. The rest of the rules are far too complicated for you to understand."

"Alright, Taffy, we believe you."

Robin glanced at Grandad with a knowing wink, and they both wondered if Taffy knew all the rules of Rugby Union.

"Alright, Robin and Grandad, now that you know the basics, let me tell you my story."

"Yes, go on, Taffy, we can hardly wait to hear it."

"Well, truth be told, I was always a happy rabbit when I was growing up. At home in Wales I ran around all day long, playing in the sunshine and eating grass.

"Sometimes, when the garden gate had been left open, I would eat the gardener's vegetables. I especially loved his carrots.

"But my passion in life was a game; can you believe that anyone can have a game as their passion in life? Well, you had better believe it, because in Wales the great passion is the game of Rugby Union. I'm not sure why it's a Welsh passion, it just is.

"The most important match of the year is when Wales play against England. I had always dreamed of getting a ticket to watch this match, but I knew it was impossible. Tickets cost *more than a hundred carrots and I would never be able to save up that many.*

"The big match day was coming up. It was to be held in Cardiff on Saturday. All of Wales was talking about it.

"Could they beat their old rivals, England?

"My mate Gareth asked me if I would like to see the match. My answer was, Yes, of course! I would do anything to be there, but I explained that I would never be able to save up enough carrots to buy a ticket.

" 'No, me neither,' said Gareth, 'but there has to be a way to get into the match. How many carrots do you have saved up?'

" 'I only have ten carrots,' I replied.

" 'Me too,' he said.

"Suddenly, I had an idea. We called all our friends from our junior rugby team and had a meeting. None of us had more than ten carrots each, so there was no way we could buy a ticket, but there were more than enough carrots to make a lot of carrot cakes!

"We got straight to work

making as many as possible, and that week we worked tirelessly, selling carrot cakes to our school friends, the teachers and relatives.

"We worked really hard and sold all the carrot cakes we had made, so on Friday afternoon we got together to add up our earnings.

"We counted all the money, and then divided it up between us. There were ninety carrots each! This was a big profit, but unfortunately, it still wasn't enough to buy the tickets. We were just ten carrots each short of being able to afford the tickets and we were really disappointed.

"We sat around with long gloomy faces, waiting for our parents to pick us up from rugby practice. None of us was really in the mood to play. We'd worked so hard, but had fallen short by such a small margin!

"The following morning, my mum woke me up very early.

" 'Get up, Taffy. We have lots to do today.'

" 'Just five more minutes, Mum,' I said.

"Come on, son, you will be late for the Wales versus England match!"

"I thought that I was dreaming!

" 'What did you say?' I asked.

" 'Well, son, the other mums and I have been talking, and seeing as you've all worked so hard, we've decided to give you the rest of the carrots you need to buy your tickets.'

"That Saturday was the best day of my life! My friends and I met at the stadium. Some of us wore daffodils - that's the national flower of Wales, you know! Gareth wore his red scarf with the three feathers in the corner.

"Gethin had a giant leek, another symbol of Wales, which doubled up as his lunch. The rest of our gang had Welsh rugby scarves and silly hats.

"It was a wonderful afternoon; the crowd were so excited, and the atmosphere was electric. It was an amazing game, full of tension for the full eighty minutes. It was wonderful to be there with all of my friends, but it felt extra special because we had all worked so hard to earn our tickets!"

"Wow, Taffy, that's a really inspiring story," said Robin. "And it's given me a great idea."

Robin was very quiet on the way home in Grandad's little red car, and Grandad knew that he was thinking up some plan.

When Robin got home, he went straight up to his room and started going through his drawers and wardrobe. He found lots of old games that he hadn't played with for years, and it gave him an idea.

He phoned Grandad to tell him about it.

"Hello, Robin. What can I do for you?"

Robin could hear Grandma complaining in the background.

"What's wrong with Grandma? She sounds a bit angry."

"Oh, don't worry, Robin, nothing much. It's just that when I got home from dropping you off I opened the bedroom window to air the place, as it seemed a bit hot and stuffy.

"It turned out that your grandma was still trying to repair the water sprinkler system in the back garden. She said that I hadn't installed it properly; something about a sprocket widget being put on upside down.

"So I went back and put everything right. I turned up the pressure so that the whole garden could get watered at the same time. Then I turned it on and came indoors for a cup of tea and some of her cake."

"So what happened next, Grandad?"

"Well, Robin, I sat in the comfy chair and fell asleep. I was woken up by your grandma shouting.

'Harry, wake up! What have you done? The sprinkler system has gone mad. You left the bedroom window open and the entire bedroom is soaked.' "

"Oh, Grandad! Is there much damage?"

"No, don't worry, Robin. With this lovely weather I'm sure that everything will be dry in no time."

"So nothing in the bedroom was damaged?" asked Robin.

"No, nothing important," said Grandad. "The only thing that was ruined was the underwater alarm clock. But Grandma didn't seem too upset about it. She just said that we would have to cancel the holiday in Atlantis."

"Grandad," said Robin, "I have to ask you for a favour. Do you think you could help me set up a stall at the car boot sale next week?"

"Oh yes, I think I can manage that, Robin. You know that you can count on me."

The following evening, Robin explained his idea to Mr Whitehouse and all the other Scouts. Then over that week, they all collected together their old toys and games.

On the next Sunday morning, they all met up bright and early. Grandad had arranged a space and borrowed a long table so that they could set up their stall.

The day started out a little slowly, and at first there weren't

many interested customers,
but as the day went on the
sales started to pick up, and by
lunchtime they had sold almost
everything!

When the car boot sale closed and the boys had finished clearing up, Mr Whitehouse made an announcement.

"Boys, I am happy to inform you that, thanks to your hard work, we have made enough money to buy some new camping equipment. So the Scout summer camp is back on!"

All the boys cheered.

"And," Grandad added with a big smile on his face, "because you have all worked so hard, Robin's Grandma has made you all an extra-special chocolate cake to celebrate."

The boys were all delighted that the Scout summer camp was able to go ahead, and as they sat around munching Grandma's delicious chocolate cake, Robin thought to himself that this was almost as good as a midnight feast!